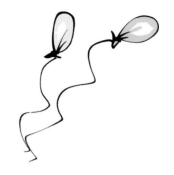

This memory book is for

....

First published in 2016
by Faber and Faber Limited
Bloomsbury House
74–77 Great Russell Street
London WC1B 3DA

Designed by Faber and Faber
Printed in China

A CIP record for this book is available from the British Library

978-0-571-32114-8

2 4 6 8 10 9 7 5 3 1

Do You Remember?

Written by Helen Docherty   Illustrated by Mark Beech

FABER & FABER

It's not easy learning to do
new things, said Mum.

But you've **always** got there in the end.

Do you remember
the first time
you got dressed
all on your own?

You wanted to choose
the perfect outfit.

Do you remember

the first time you used the potty?

You carried it into the kitchen
to show us all, you were **so proud**.

Do you remember

the first time you jumped
with both feet together?

You landed
right in the
middle of a
puddle...

and Grandpa got wet!

But we all clapped anyway.

Do you remember

the first time you

 sang a song?

Everybody on the bus got to hear you sing it

over and **OVER** again!

Do you remember

the first time you

fed yourself with

a spoon?

You were watching us the **whole** time

...and copying us **very** carefully.

Do you remember . . .

the

first

time

you

walked

 on

your

own?

We were both there cheering you along.

Do you remember

the first time you

crawled?

You were **SO** determined

to get hold of that balloon.

Do you remember

the first time you sat up on your own?

I gave you a tambourine to bash

...but you tried to eat it instead.

Do you remember

the first time you tried to talk to me?

You made a lovely cooing noise.

 It sounded like you really wanted

to tell me something.

Do you remember

the first time you smiled at me?

I was talking to you while you

lay on your blanket

...and suddenly you beamed up at me.

Do you remember

the **first** time you **grabbed** hold of my finger?

You squeezed it so tightly
I thought you would
never let go.

You see . . .

Everything you've

ever wanted to do,

you've always

found a way to do it.